YAYATI

DEVAYANI WAS THE ONLY DAUGHTER OF SHUKRACHARYA, THE PRECEPTOR OF VRISHA-PARVA, KING OF THE ASURAS. UNFORTUNATELY SHE WAS A SPOILT, WILFUL GIRL AS HER FATHER DOTED ON HER, INDULGING HER EVERY WHIM AND FANCY.

ONE MORNING, SHARMISHTHA, THE ASURA PRINCESS, CALLED ON SHUKRACHARYA.

"HOLY ONE, WE ARE GOING TO THE GARDEN OF THE GANDHARVAS* IN THE FOREST, TO SWIM IN THE LAKE THERE. MAY WE TAKE DEVAYANI WITH US?"

"DO SO BY ALL MEANS. BUT TAKE GOOD CARE OF HER."

"I CERTAINLY WILL, HOLY ONE! I KNOW HOW MUCH YOU LOVE HER."

SHARMISHTHA AND DEVAYANI LEFT THE ASHRAM WITH THEIR FRIENDS.

*CELESTIAL MUSICIANS, A CLASS OF 'DEMI-GODS'

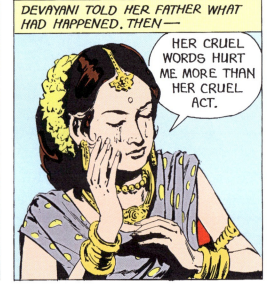

Her anger appeased, Devayani and Shukracharya returned to the ashram.

A few days later, Devayani went once again to the same forest with Sharmishtha and the other maids.

Catch me!

A FEW DAYS LATER, YAYATI MARRIED DEVAYANI.

WHEN IT WAS TIME FOR THEM TO TAKE LEAVE OF SHUKRACHARYA —

YAYATI, TAKE CARE OF DEVAYANI. SHE IS DEARER TO ME THAN LIFE.

I WILL, REVERED ONE.

KEEP HER HAPPY. NEVER HURT HER BY YOUR WORDS OR DEEDS.

I ASSURE YOU, I WON'T, HOLY ONE.

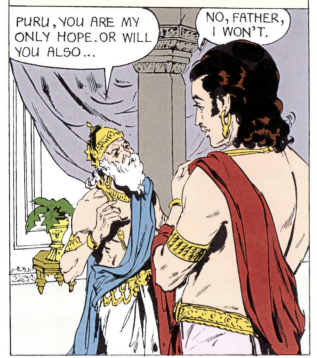